Alfred the Curious

Story by Jenny Hellen
Illustrations by Mal Liddell

Contents

Chapter 1

Preparing for Battle

Alfred was running down the spiral stairs of Lord Edward's castle, when he heard the pounding noise of horses' hooves. Through the narrow slit in the tower wall, he could see men on horses, galloping hard and fast. They were coming towards the castle!

Alfred realised it was Lord Edward and his knights. But behind them, clouds of dust rose higher and higher. Lord William and his army were coming after Lord Edward!

The two lords had been fighting over the castle for a long time.

Alfred was scared and excited at the same time. There'd be no more running messages for Lady Eleanor today, and no more French lessons; being a page could be so boring. But now there'd be some action!

When Alfred reached the courtyard, people were running in all directions. The animals were being shut into their pens. The children were being hurried inside. The archers were racing up the stairs to take their positions along the parapet. Foot soldiers were getting their lances and pikes, and heading towards the gatehouse.

The gatehouse keepers were ready to winch the drawbridge up once Lord Edward and his knights were safely inside.

Alfred saw the archers above the gatehouse getting their bows ready to fire on the enemy. Along the parapet, foot soldiers were preparing huge pots of boiling water. They would pour the water on any of Lord William's men who came too close to the castle walls.

Alfred wanted to watch the gatehouse keepers, to see how quickly they could move the gigantic winches that raised the drawbridge. But he felt a hand on his shoulder. It was Bartholomew, Lord Edward's squire.

"Alfred, you shouldn't be here, it's too dangerous! And you've got work to do. You're supposed to be in the stables. Come on!" said Bartholomew. He pulled Alfred away from the gatehouse, and sent him across the courtyard.

Thud ... Thud ... Thud ... The thundering of the horses' hooves shook the ground beneath them.

Thwat ... Thwat ... Thwat ... Arrows screamed in and bounced off the inside walls of the castle.

The battle for the castle had begun.

Chapter 2

The Battle for Lord Edward's Castle

Lord Edward rode at full speed into the courtyard. When the last of his knights had crossed the drawbridge, it was closed behind them. Bartholomew took the horse's reins as Lord Edward leapt down. Without stopping to look around, Lord Edward dashed straight up to the parapet, where archers were already firing arrows back at the enemy.

Alfred began to feel scared. What if Lord William's army broke through and took over the castle? What would become of his family and friends?

Then Alfred remembered he had work to do. Alto, Lord Edward's horse, had to be cooled down. Bartholomew led the horse over to Alfred and helped him take the saddle off, then went to join Lord Edward on the parapet. Alfred was left to rub Alto down.

When he was finished, Alfred was supposed to join the other children inside the castle. Instead, he crept up to the parapet. Alfred was desperate to see what the battle was like — perhaps he could even be a part of it!

"What on earth are you doing here, boy?" boomed Lord Edward's voice.

"I just wanted to see the battle," squeaked Alfred. "Maybe I could do something to help?"

Lord Edward looked annoyed. "Very well — Bartholomew, make use of him. Take him down to the storeroom and get more arrows. The archers have almost run out."

Chapter 3

A Strange Noise

"Follow me," Bartholomew snapped at Alfred. His voice sounded hard, but he was not angry. He understood Alfred's curiosity.

They bounded down the stairs, two at a time, until they reached the storeroom. They grabbed armfuls of arrows — as many as they could carry. But, then, just as they were leaving, Alfred thought he heard something odd.

"What's that noise?" Alfred whispered.

Bartholomew shrugged. "Probably just rats," he said. "Come on! We've got to hurry back."

But the noise grew louder.

"Wait!" whispered Alfred. "Listen!"

They both stood very still and put their ears to the wall. They could hear a kind of scraping sound.

"It must be Lord William's men trying to tunnel through into the castle!" Alfred gasped. "I've heard they do that sometimes!"

Bartholomew looked at Alfred in surprise.

Alfred went on so quickly his words ran together. "If they tunnel under the wall, they could light a fire under it. The fire would make the wall collapse. Then Lord William and his soldiers would be able to walk right into the castle. We would all be doomed!"

"We must tell Lord Edward immediately," said Bartholomew.

They raced up the stairs with their loads of arrows. Alfred's legs wanted to stop and rest, but he wouldn't let them. There was no way he was going to miss this! He pushed on and up after Bartholomew, until, finally, they reached the top.

Lord Edward looked grim when he heard the news. He knew what could happen if Lord William's men tunnelled under the castle wall.

"Alfred, Bartholomew, join the foot soldiers," he ordered. "Scout the length of the parapet. Look out for anything unusual. The tunnellers will have built a wooden hut for protection somewhere beside the castle wall. It could be covered with branches and leaves, so it may be hard to see. But we must find them — and fast!"

Chapter 4

The Search

Alfred could feel his heart thumping. Rocks were flying through the air, and arrows were whizzing over his head. He strained to see over the parapet.

And then he saw it!

"There it is!" shouted Alfred. "I can see the edge of their hut. It has animal hides covering it, as well as tree branches."

"Good work!" Bartholomew said, sounding impressed. "Now, run and tell Lord Edward."

Alfred raced back along the parapet as fast as he could.

Chapter 5

Retreat

Lord Edward knew what to do. "Archers, fire flaming arrows at it! Foot soldiers, drop the heaviest stones on it! We will destroy this hut and send them packing!"

Alfred watched as the hut went up in flames. He hoped that no one hiding underneath had been hurt. Alfred hated that about war. His father had once been badly hurt in a battle. It had taken him months to get well again.

Alfred knew they had to fight to protect their homes and their lives — but he wished it could be done without anyone getting hurt.

Lord William's army started to retreat. With their secret plan destroyed, they had to give up.

Alfred knew how lucky they were that the siege hadn't gone on for days, or weeks, or even months. But he also knew that the enemy would be back ... eventually.

Chapter 6

A Celebration

That night, to celebrate the victory, there was a feast in the Great Hall. Everyone was there — the knights, the squires and even the pages. They had the best food and drink, and the court jester made them all laugh with his silly jokes and songs.

After dinner, Lord Edward called Alfred over to his table.

"Alfred, you are very curious. Always being in places you shouldn't, and looking at things that don't concern you. That can get you into trouble. But it also makes you think and investigate.

And, thanks to you, today we have had
a great victory. I think you may be a
great knight some day. But, for now,
I am pleased to have you as my page."

Alfred felt so proud! Yes — he would like to be a knight some day. The excitement, the thrill, the danger!

That night, as he drifted off to sleep, Alfred dreamed of riding on his own great horse, leading other knights into battle to fight for his king ...